Tall Tales of Old India from a Very, Very, Very Long Time Ago

CROW, MOUSE, TURTLE, DEER
The Panchatantra Book Two Retold

Narindar Uberoi Kelly
Illustrated by Meagan Jenigen

For My Daughter Kieran Kelly Holmes

Order this book online at www.trafford.com
or email orders@trafford.com

Most Trafford titles are also available at major online book retailers.

Printed in the United States of America.

ISBN: 978-1-4907-4030-0 (sc)
978-1-4907-4031-7 (e)

Trafford rev. 07/07/2014

 www.trafford.com

North America & international
toll-free: 1 888 232 4444 (USA & Canada)
fax: 812 355 4082

Note To The Reader

I fell in love with these stories as a tween who stumbled across them in a library at a time when my family were refugees as a result of the partition of India between what is now Pakistan and India. I suppose part of the attraction of the stories was escape from the realities of being homeless in a part of India that seemed a different country, with people speaking different languages and eating food quite unlike anything I was used to. But the stories helped me by giving me some insight into what and why my parents were trying to teach me—and some appreciation for what I was resisting in a world turned upside down by our narrow escape from the violence and turmoil of our loss of home and country.

I decided I wanted my grandchildren to have access to these stories that meant so much to me, but in a language that they could easily understand. As I adapted the stories for modern readers, it occurred to me one of the great strengths of the Panchatantra (literally the five books) derives from what at first seems the sheer nonsense of listening in to animals talking like humans. Yet this absurd conceit of animals chatting and arguing and telling stories immediately establishes a strangely safe distance between the reader and these creatures. And even more strangely, we are transformed into observers and compatriots in their struggles with thorny issues of friendship, collaboration, conflict and ambition. If I was particularly taken with these tales at a time of vulnerability and uncertainty in my life, readers approaching and experiencing adolescence and young maturity (when does that process end?) are in some sense similarly adrift and puzzled by the strange new land of adulthood. Readers of these tales are assumed to be much like I was--expatriates operating in a new landscape they don't fully understand.

The genius of these stories is their relentless unwillingness to whitewash or romanticize adult life. They depict the ignoble as well as the noble, cruelty and deceit as well as honor, foolishness as much as cunning, deception as rampant as honesty. They show the underside as well as glimpses of fulfillment in adult life. The stories unveil the contradictory nature of adult life, its tensions, risks and dangers as well as its rewards. And it accomplishes this through the disorienting welter of stories within stories that pile up on each other to convey a kind of confusion that forms a powerful antidote to other literary forms designed to convey wisdom—like preaching, teaching, telling people what to do. Out of this confusion, somehow wisdom can escape as a form of deeper appreciation of the perils and tensions and value of leading a good life.

Narindar Uberoi Kelly

TALL TALES OF OLD INDIA

There was a king called Immortal-Power who lived in a fabulous city which had everything. He had three sons. They were truly ignorant. The King saw that they could not figure things out and did not want to learn. They hated school. So the King asked a very wise man to wake up their brains. The wise man, a Brahmin named Sharma, took the three Princes to his home. Every day he told them stories that taught the Princes lessons on how to live intelligently. To make sure they would never forget he made them learn the stories by heart. The second set of teaching tales Sharma told were:

Crow, Mouse, Turtle, Deer

Sharma began

"Four friends, all poor, but having
Common sense and learning,
Lived well together than
Each could have separately."

"What do you mean?" asked the three Princes, and Sharma told this story.

CROW, MOUSE, TURTLE DEER

The Panchatantra Book Two Retold

Narindar Uberoi Kelly

Illustrated by Meagan Jenigen

Crow, Mouse, Turtle, Deer

Introduction

INTRODUCTION

The purpose of these stories has always been to teach basic knowledge and wisdom that makes for a better life. Each of the five 'books' in the original were organized around a theme: Loss of Friends, Making Friends, War or Peace, Loss of Gains, Ill-considered Action.

Book Two, here titled simply 'Crow, Mouse, Turtle, Deer', deals with four friends: how they meet, how they get to know each other, how they become friends even though they are different species (one might even say, natural enemies) and how they help each other to survive and thrive when life becomes difficult.

The foundation story of the book is the account of the four friends, their past and present. Sharma, the tutor engaged by the King to wake up the brains of his three sons, the Princes, so they could learn to live and govern wisely, tells of how a Crow named Sight first meets a Mouse named Smart and how they become friends.

Sight observes and learns from the experience of a group of doves and from Keen, the Dove King, about the effectiveness and value of cooperation and friendship. Smart was a friend of Keen and frees the ensnared doves from certain death. Sight, now appreciating the value of friendship, seeks it from Smart. In return, when fortune takes a nasty turn and they both have to flee their home city, they take refuge with Sight's friend, a turtle named Sense. The three friends then tell stories about hardship and friendship until Deer arrives and seeks their friendship which they eventually offer him.

The main or *frame* story told by Crow, Mouse, Turtle, Deer as they build their relationship is separated in this presentation from the *stand-alone or nesting* stories that are cited in the frame story. The frame story is to be found on the left hand pages of the open book where the text is enclosed within a 'frame'. The stand-alone or nesting stories are told on the right hand pages of the book. This allows parents reading aloud to young children, young adults, or adults of any age, to choose whether they want to read or ignore the often lesson-laden frame story in its entirety or pick and choose one or more of the nesting or stand-alone stories. For the curious or the purist, the book can be read in its entirety left to right on the open pages to experience the original design of this book of stories.

Book Two is an elaborate tale of true friendship that flourishes despite the vastly differing natures of the individuals and the travails they face. The strengths of each friend make the group strong and effective in addressing the challenges they face.

Crow, Mouse, Turtle, Deer

Crow Observes the Doves

In a big banyan tree in a famous city called Sunrise lived a crow named Sight. One morning, as he started to go in search of food, he spied a hunter approaching his tree. The Hunter looked fearsome and ugly as he came nearer carrying his snare and his rod. Sight got ready to keep close watch as the Hunter picked a spot, spread his net, and scattered some grain. But the birds in the banyan tree who had listened to Sight's advice did not get tempted by the bird-seed and kept very still and quiet.

But the leader of a flock of doves, named Keen, disregarded Sight's warning. He had seen the grain beneath the tree from a long way off and brought his followers with him to feed as he alighted. Of course, he and his doves were ensnared. Clearly, Keen had made a big mistake. Everyone makes mistakes. But Keen kept his head. He immediately rallied his doves "We must all work together with one purpose, we must all fly up in unison, and carry the net with us, and we will all be saved. Remember the 'one-belly-two-mouth' birds?" "Tell us" requested the doves, and Keen told them this story.

Peculiar Birds

By a small lake lived a couple of peculiar birds who had a common belly but two separate heads and mouths. One day, one head found some delicious berries. The second head wanted some too so it said "Give me half the berries." But the first refused to share. So the second head got really angry and ate a plant that it knew was poisonous. Sure enough, since they had one common belly, both died.

*

When the doves heard the story, they immediately got together, worked without fear, in complete unison, flew in a tight formation, and managed to carry off the snare with them. The Hunter was amazed but figured that the dove's unity would not last long and that he would eventually get his prey. So the Hunter pursued the doves flying overhead.

Keen, however, saw the Hunter coming after them below, guessed his purpose, and again, keeping his head, directed his flock to fly over hilly areas with dense undergrowth that would be hard for the Hunter to cross.

Watching all this, Sight, was surprised both by the Hunter's persistence and Keen's reactions. He was very impressed by how Keen was leading his doves to safety and began to follow to see what would happen next.

Eventually, the Hunter realized that he would not be able to keep up with the flock and turned back towards his home bemoaning the fact that he had not only lost his catch but the snare by which he supported his family. Fate had certainly done him in.

Seeing the Hunter give up his pursuit, Keen directed his flock of doves to turn towards Sunrise City. His great friend, the mouse called Smart, lived there. "He will cut through the snare and set us free" he told his doves egging them on.

Upon the arrival of the whole flock at his doorstep, and the noise of their wings flapping in unison, Smart was quite concerned. So he asked for the identity of his visitors while he kept himself well-hidden. Once Keen had assured Smart that he was a friend in trouble, Smart welcomed him and wanted to know what happened. "Fate has its way" answered Keen.

When Smart began to cut through the net nearest to him, Keen objected and said "Please cut the bonds of my followers first. As the saying goes, *the King who honors his retainers more than their due always has servants when his money is lost*. Besides, if something goes wrong and your teeth begin to hurt, I would lose everything seeing my attendants suffering and would go to hell." Smart cut the bonds of all the doves and they were free to fly home.

That is why they say that a man can make gains with help of friends even when the going gets difficult. So get friends and think of them as treasure.

Crow and Mouse Become Friends

Sight understood what Smart had really been saying. Goodness, this is one intelligent mouse he thought. Perhaps I should try and make friends with him? Even though I am naturally suspicious, I should learn to trust others for they do say that even those who are self-sufficient should seek friends who can be invaluable. Having thought things through, Sight approached the entrance to Smart's home. Smart had the equivalent of a rabbit's warren or a mole's burrow: lots of connected underground tunnels. It had many entrances and many exits so that, if in danger, Smart and his followers could enter and leave in many ways and would not be an easy catch.

Sight called "Smart, please come out." Staying hidden, Smart asked "Who is it?" "My name is Sight. I am a crow" replied Sight. Immediately Smart became concerned. His visitor was of a kind hostile to mice so he said "Please Leave." But the Crow was persistent "I come in good faith. Please talk to me a while." "I see no good coming from talking to you". In answer the Crow explained that he had learned how bright and competent Smart was and how he had readily freed the doves. Sight continued "There may come a day, when I could also be caught like your friend, Keen, and I would need a friend like you. Please let us be friends, even if we are different and seen as natural enemies."

But Smart still hesitated "You eat and I am food. How can I trust you enough to be friends?" "After all" he continued "friendship between un-equals never works. Ordinary enemies can be dealt with but natural enemies are life-long. Think of the hostility between snake and mongoose, dogs and cats, lions and elephants, crows and owls, herbivores and carnivores, gods and devils, scholars and idiots, rival wives, saints and sinners." "But" the Crow cried, "this doesn't make sense, does it? A man becomes a friend for cause and grows hostile for cause. So the prudent make friends, not foes. Don't give cause for a foe."

So the discussion on friendship and ethics continued between Sight, the Crow, and Smart, the Mouse. In the end, each was convinced of the intelligence and common sense of the other, each had won the confidence of the other, and each decided to give friendship between creatures of a different kind, such as they were, a chance.

Having agreed to be friends, Sight resumed his search for food. He flew over a nearby forest and came upon the remains of a buffalo killed by a tiger. He not only ate his fill but took some choice pieces to give his new found friend, Smart. When he presented the meat to the Mouse, he found that his friend had also been gathering corn and rice to share with his friend, the Crow. The two were very pleased with the gifts given and received. As they say, friendship grows if you do six things: receive, give, listen, talk, dine and entertain. By doing these the Crow and the Mouse became fast friends.

Crow and Mouse Go to See Turtle

Time passed. One day, when a long developing drought gripped the countryside, and famine could be seen round the corner, Sight became very depressed and said to Smart: "Things are getting really bad. The people are starving and instead of putting birdseed out in their yards, they are setting traps to catch birds for food. I haven't been caught yet but could be next. So I have decided to leave this area." "Where will you go?" asked Smart. Sight replied "In the far West is a great lake surrounded by dense woods. My dear friend Sense, a turtle, lives there. He will feed me fish and we will enjoy good fellowship with good conversation and good cheer, and I will be able to forget the disaster spreading here."

"Given the current situation, I will follow you because I too have a great sorrow." "What is it?" asked Sight but Smart simply said "It is a long story. I will tell you when we reach where we are going." "We really should travel together but I go by air and you by ground" pointed out Sight. "Perhaps, you should ride on me?" "Please carry me gently" requested Smart. "I know all eight flights" replied Sight, "a long steady cruise, an upward dart, a smooth horizontal, a sharp downward, a straight rise, a clear circling, a defined zigzag, and a short flight. Not to worry, I will get you to our destination in comfort."

When Sense saw them as they reached the lake, he wondered at the strange bedfellows. When he understood who his visitors were, he welcomed them. As they sat down to dinner after the usual pleasantries, Sense asked "So, who is this mouse?" Sight explained that Smart was his very dear friend whose virtues were too numerous to count but that he had a great sorrow which had brought him on a visit to Sense. "Pray, tell us the story of your great sorrow" asked Sense and Smart began the story of his great loss.

Mouse Loses Everything

Mouse began his story: "You have heard of a city called Sunrise. I used to live there in a hermit's cell. The Hermit, called Missing Ear for he had lost it in an accident early on, used to beg for alms. When he got home, he would eat his fill of the best food he had been given, and leave some for his servant in the begging bowl which he used to hang on a peg. I could always reach the bowl no matter how high he hung it and I lived quite well on it.

One day, the Hermit had a visitor, a holy man named Venerable. Missing Ear paid him due deference and welcomed him in. As the guest sat recounting a particularly worthy tale, Missing Ear had to get up quite often to tap the begging bowl to keep me from eating all the food in it. Annoyed at the interruptions, Venerable decided to leave and go where he was more welcome. He rightly pointed out that a true friend always gives full attention and talks wholeheartedly. "You are not really listening to me." said Venerable. "You are too proud and yet only a lowly hermit. I am leaving."

Missing Ear was upset. "Please, please don't leave. I only *seem* inattentive for I must keep banging the begging bowl to keep the mouse from eating all the food I have saved for my guest. This mouse is really very clever and I have to be ever vigilant. He seems to best me no matter what I try to do to keep the food safe." "Have you found the mouse hole?" asked Venerable. "No" was the reply. "Surely" continued the holy man "the mouse hole entrance must be over his hoard. And it must be the smell from it that makes the mouse so clever and frisky. The smell of wealth and its enjoyment increases with the hoard. But there must be a reason why this mouse can always outwit you. As they say, if Mrs. Shrewd was bargaining hulled grains for un-hulled, she must have had a good reason." "How was that?" asked Missing Ear, and Venerable told this story.

Mrs. Shrewd and Her Bargain

Once, Venerable needed a place to stay in the rainy season and asked a Brahmin for help. The Brahmin gave him shelter and Venerable lived there for a while and continued to do his pious duties. One day he woke early and overheard the Brahmin say to his Wife: "Tomorrow is the winter solstice, a big day for us, so I will go to a different village to get donations. Please give any Brahmin who comes to our door looking for alms as much food as you can in honor of the Sun." "But" the Wife retorted "How can I donate food when we have so little for ourselves? Why should I feed any beggar?" The Brahmin was upset. "You know the saying, even if you only have a mouthful, give half to the needy. The reward in heaven is as much as if you gave away half of untold riches. Remember, the greedy jackal killed by the bow?" "No" said his Wife, and the Brahmin told this story.

The Ill-fated Jackal That Tried To Hoard

A hunter set out hunting in a forest. He soon saw a boar and quickly drew his arrow and shot him. But the boar managed to gore the hunter in the stomach so that both died in pain. Later that same day, a hungry Jackal came by and saw the unexpected kill and realizing his good luck, decided to feast on it very slowly so as to sustain himself for many days. He would carefully hoard his find. As the saying goes, wise men sip fine wine to savor it to the full. So the jackal, with apparent good foresight, began with the sinew attached to the bow. The gut string broke when stretched too far and snapped back hard so that the bow-tip pierced through the roof of his mouth into the Jackal's head. He also died from pain.

"The point is" continued the Brahmin, *"five things are preordained before birth: length of life, fate, wealth, learning and tomb."* "OK" the Wife replied. "I have some sesame grain left which I will grind up into flour so I can feed any Brahmin who comes to our door." Hearing his wife promise to do the right thing, the Brahmin left as planned for a nearby village to get donations.

The Wife, known as Mrs. Shrewd, proceeded to soften the sesame grains in boiling water, hulled them, put them in a dish and put them out in the hot sun, and went about doing her other chores. A stray dog came by house and started eating from the dish. "Oh dear, Oh dear" said the Wife to herself. *When fate turns against us it cannot be stopped.* The sesame grains are no longer fit to eat. What shall I do? Perhaps I will take them to a neighbor's house and offer to exchange un-hulled sesame for hulled. Anyone will like such a deal. "As it happened" Venerable continued "Mrs. Shrewd went to a house where I was a guest. There, the housewife, of course, took the deal but when her husband came home and she told him about it, he immediately told her to throw the hulled sesame away. 'Mrs. Shrewd is too astute to give anything away without profit. She must have had a reason for such a deal'.

"Likewise, let us see if we can figure out why the Mouse always gets the food in your begging bowl. Do you have a digging tool?" asked Venerable. "I have a pick-axe" said Missing Ear. "Let's get up early in the morning and follow the Mouse tracks to his hoard."

Smart was deeply upset when he heard these words. "This will spell ruin for me. This holy man, Venerable, is one brainy Brahmin. He will find my stash of riches for sure." So he quickly changed course and ran off with his followers to a new hole. But fate was against him and Venerable was able to find everything he was looking for with the pick-axe and the neighbor's cat. "Between them" Smart went on "they destroyed my home and my food stores, scared off my followers, and stole my riches. I departed alone and dejected. My vigor had been kept alive by my sense of well-being and knowledge that I was wealthy. Without it, I was but a poor mouse without a following.

As the saying goes, *when a man is bowed down by poverty and an unkind fate, his friends turn to foes and love to hate. Beggary is as bad as death itself.* What course is still open to me? *Living by stealing or robbing is accursed as is living always on another's charity.*

So, after a long time, I decided to try and reclaim my property even if I died in the attempt. My attempt failed but I escaped death because my time was not up yet. Predestination, as always, played its part. That is why they say *a man will get his due and even the Gods cannot prevent it.*" "How can that be?" asked the Crow and the Turtle, and the Mouse told this story.

Man Will Get What Is Due Him

There was a trader named Money whose son lived at home. One day, the Son bought a book which had only one line written in it. "Man will get what is due him." The Father asked his Son "How much did you pay for this?" "A hundred silver coins" replied the Son. The Father, Money, became enraged at his son's inability to grasp the value of silver coins. "How can you ever make a living if you spend without considering the return! You had better leave and try earning your keep."

The Son had no choice but to leave and go far away from home. He took his book with him and got quite obsessed with what was written in it. So much so that when anyone in the city where he finally ended up asked him something he always replied with "Man will get what is due him." So he got the nickname, Pay Back.

Meanwhile, it so happened that a Princess named Moonlight was taking a stroll in the park with a girlfriend and saw a Prince riding by. She was instantly smitten and asked her girl friend to arrange an introduction and meeting. The Girlfriend approached the Prince and gave him the message that the Princess Moonlight had fallen in love with him and that he should visit her. "You can climb up to the Princess' balcony by means of the ladder that I will place nearby for your use." The Prince agreed and left.

By nightfall, however, the Prince decided not to go on the clandestine visit. It would not be honorable to sneak off at night to meet with a Princess. However, as it happened, Pay Back came by on his nightly wanderings, noticed the ladder and climbed up to the balcony. Princess Moonlight, convinced that he was the right man, treated him with affection, respect and great generosity. "You are definitely the love of my life. I will never have another. Now I have told you everything about myself. Why don't you talk to me?" "Man will get what is due him." He replied. Stunned by Pay Back's response, the Princess quickly sent him away.

Pay Back went to a derelict temple building and went to sleep on the floor in a corner. Presently, a policeman showed up who had a tryst in the deserted temple with a woman not his wife. When the Policeman saw Pay Back, he asked "Who are you?" to which Pay Back replied with his usual "Man will get what is due him". The Policeman was shocked to hear such words and wanting to hush up the whole matter suggested that Pay Back go to his house and go to sleep in his bed. Pay Back, of course, accepted the generous offer but when he reached the Policeman's house, he mistakenly got into the bed of the Policeman's daughter Naughty.

Now the Daughter had arranged to spend the night with a lover and so accepted Pay Back as the lover and therefor husband-to-be. Later, she said to him. "You are very quiet today. Why are you not talking to me?" "Man will get what is due him" came the reply. Naughty decided she had better send him packing and did so.

As Pay Back walked along a brightly lit city street, he met a young man on his way to get married and joined in the procession of friends and relatives. They soon reached the bride-to-be's house all decked out with party tents and wedding decorations. But, Heavens! Just then a rogue elephant appeared and ran amuck destroying everything in sight. The guests fled, even the bridegroom. Pay Back saw the terrified bride hide in a corner and ran to her help. Somehow he managed to protect her from the elephant who took off soon enough.

When everyone came back, they saw the bride-to-be in Pay Back's arms. The bridegroom-to-be confronted her father in anger. "First you promised your daughter to me and then handed her to another man!" The Father turned to his daughter "What is the meaning of this?" and she replied "This man saved my life. I will not have another man hold my hand as long as I live." Everyone who heard her words was taken with the story and quickly told everyone else. By mid-morning, the Princess Moonlight, Naughty, even the King arrived on the scene where a great crowd was now gathered.

"What is going on?" the King asked Pay Back. "Speak without fear." "Man will get what is due him" replied Pay Back. Hearing the words again, the Princess said "No one can break this law. Not even the Gods." Then Naughty said "I am not surprised or sad", and the bride-to-be said "No one should take what is mine."

The King eventually arrived at the truth by piecing together the various accounts of everyone involved. He was rather impressed by Pay Back, gave him his own daughter in marriage and made him the Crown Prince since he did not have a son of his own. Everybody lived happily thereafter.

*

After the Mouse finished telling the story, he went on "I learned a lot from Pay Back, that he truly believed that most people do get their just desserts, but I also recovered from my own money madness. I had forgotten that my hoard of gold wasn't the only property I had lost. I had also lost contentment. Anyway", he concluded, "it was at this time of my great sorrow that Sight needed my help. And when Sight decided to visit you, Sense, I too tagged along although I am still upset about leaving my home and country."

Turtle Tries To Cheer Mouse

"Don't lose heart, my dear fellow" said Sense. "*You are intelligent and with wise action you can make any country your own country just as the lion makes any forest his kingdom. We must always be energetic because man and beast, friends, and even money are drawn to vigor. Competence is at home with the brave and the sturdy because they live an active life. There is no difference between native and foreign country for those who are competent and competitive.* Smart, today your purse may be light but with your brains and energy and resolution, you can fill it up again. *The intelligent man enjoys his money by spending it wisely or giving it away to the needy. Only the miser hoards it and so may as well not have it.* Always remember, *there is no treasure like charity, no wealth like contentment, no gem like character and no wish like health.* You are still rich. But remember also that *some are born to enjoy the pleasures that money provides but some are born merely to save it.* Think of the simple Weaver." "Tell me" requested Smart, and Sense told the story:

Weaver Named Plain

There was once a Weaver named Plain who lived in a good-sized city with his wife. He wove beautiful fabrics that people made into clothes that were prized by many. He worked hard but Plain never seemed to earn more than a modest living. Yet he saw others who were not as good as he was at weaving but who made lots of money. Plain got more and more discouraged and dissatisfied until one day he announced to his wife that he was going to another city. "My dear" the Wife said "you are making a mistake. Money doesn't come to people who travel! What fate has willed always follows. The Doer and the Deed are as intertwined as sunlight and shade no matter where you are." But Plain disagreed. "A deed only happens with effort. I must leave here." So he went to Expanding City and worked there for three years. His work sold better and when he had saved three hundred gold coins, he decided to return home.

On his way back he had to cross fairly dense woods. To be safe, he climbed a tall banyan tree at sunset and went to sleep. He was woken by two shrouded human figures arguing with each other. Figure One said "Doer, you know you must prevent Plain from ever having more than a modest living. Why did you allow him to get three hundred gold coins?" Figure Two replied "Listen, Deed. I must reward enterprise so I had to let him have the money. What happens next is your problem. You can take it away." Hearing them, Plain quickly checked his purse and found it empty. He was truly dejected because his hard-earned money had disappeared in a flash and he could not face going home to his wife empty-handed. So Plain went back to Expanding City. There he worked doubly hard and managed to save five hundred gold coins in just one year. So he started for home again but by a different road.

At sunset, he found himself under the same banyan tree as before and was very upset. But he climbed up it again with his money purse and went to sleep. Again, he awoke to the same two Figures arguing. Figure One said "Doer, why did you give Plain five hundred gold coins? He is not supposed to have more than a modest living." Again, Figure Two replied "Deed, I have to give to the enterprising. The final consequence is your affair. Why blame me?" Again, Plain looked in his money bag and found it empty. He couldn't bear it any longer and decided to hang himself from the branch of the accursed banyan tree. However, just when he was about to hang, a third figure appeared and said "Don't be so hasty. I am the one who takes your money and do not allow you more than a modest living. Just go home. But because you have touched me, I will grant you one wish." "Just make me rich" requested Plain. "What on earth will you do with money you cannot enjoy or give away for you are to have no use of it except for living modestly?" "I want it even if I can't use it" answered Plain. "Think of the greedy jackal and the hang-balls." "How was that?" asked Figure Three and Plain told this story.

Hang-Ball and the Greedy Jackal

In a small town near some woods there lived a very virile young bull nick-named Hang-Ball because of his very large and very prominent testicles. One day, a female jackal named Nagger, pointed out the balls to her husband. She thought they would taste good and so asked her husband to see if he could get them for her. She thought that they would fall down soon enough of their own accord and so forced her husband to follow the bull around. The Jackal, named Easy Led, thought it was a fool's errand. "Maybe the balls will fall one day, but maybe they will not. I would rather not go after the bull in the hope of getting a treat. I think it is much better if we stay here with the surety of catching mice regularly for our dinner." But greedy Nagger insisted. "Perseverance will pay off" she said. Easy Led followed the bull for fifteen long years egged on by his wife, Nagger. In the end, both had to admit it was time to give up and accept that if the balls had not fallen until now, they would not fall in the future."

*

Having told the story, Plain expanded "If I am rich I will become an object of desire." Still, Figure Three hesitated. "Go back to Expanding City," he said "and observe closely two sons of merchants named Penny-Hide and Penny-Fling. After you have done so, you may ask for the nature of one or the other" and Figure Three disappeared.

Back went Plain to Expanding City and searched out Penny-Hide's house. When he arrived there he sat down in the courtyard to see what would happen. He was given a meager meal but no kindness and went to sleep on an uncomfortable cot out of doors.

In the middle of the night he heard the same two figures that had appeared before. Figure One asked "Doer, why are you making more expense for Penny-Hide by making him feed Plain?" "Deed, you cannot blame me. I have to account for earnings and expenses. The final result is your affair." Plain left Penny-Hide's home, hungry, and went to Penny-Fling's the next morning. He was welcomed warmly and given not just food but clothes as well as a comfortable bed. That night Plain again saw the figures and listened in. "Doer, Penny-Fling has just gotten himself deeper into debt by being so hospitable to Plain." "Deed", said Figure Two "I had to do it. The final consequence is your affair." At dawn the next day, a policeman showed up with money by the King's favor and gave it to Penny-Fling. Plain pondered upon what he had observed and when next Figure Three appeared, asked to be made a person like Penny-Fling who enjoyed and shared his money even when it was meager.

"So there is little point in spending time in worry and woe for fate will tap good or bad for me and you" continued Sense. *"There is no penance like patience, no peace like contentment, no pleasure like sharing, no joy like mercy, no meaning like friends.* But enough of preaching. Please stay here in friendship with me as long as you like."

Sight also joined in the conversation adding "You are so right, Sense, so wise. As they say, *what good is manhood that doesn't make the sorrowful secure, what good wealth that doesn't help the poor, what good action that doesn't result in betterment, what good life that doesn't bring approval."*

The Deer Arrives

Just then a deer named Speed arrived at the lakeshore where the three friends were talking. He was panting with thirst and trembling from fear. Immediately the three friends made themselves scarce: Sight flew up into a tree, Smart went into a hole in the ground, Sense dived into the lake.

After a while, Sight flew off to scout for any lurking danger and finding no indication came back to reassure his friends. "All is quiet" he announced, "The deer just came to the lake for water." So all three friends gathered as before and invited the deer to join them. Speed thought things through: the turtle can't hurt me out of the water and the mouse and crow eat only carrion. So he joined them.

"Sense asked "What brings you here?" "I am tired of a life without love" replied Speed. "I have been hounded most of my life by hunters and their dogs and it is only fear that gives me the speed to out run them. So I came to this place looking for water and hoping to find friendship." Sense said "We are small and you are big. It is unnatural for us to be friends. We would never be able to do you any favors." "Why are you selling yourself short" went on Speed. "Remember the mice that set the elephants free?" "How was that?" asked Sense, and Speed told this story.

Mice Set the Elephants Free

Once there was an old city that became so run down that people left it. Soon afterwards it became a city where a colony of mice began to live and thrive.

Time passed and the mice multiplied many fold. One day an Elephant-King came that way with his very large herd. As the elephants tramped through Mouse City on their way to a lake where there was plenty of water, they destroyed lots and lots of mice. When they had gone, the surviving mice gathered to figure out a way to prevent such carnage happening ever again, for they worried that if the elephants came that way again, the mouse race would be extinguished. The mice eventually decided that the best way to proceed would be to go to the lake and negotiate a truce with the elephants. When they appeared before the Elephant-King, they bowed low and respectfully petitioned him. "O King, we have suffered such destruction at the hands of your followers that we fear extinction if you pass through our city again. So we come here to beg for your mercy and request that you travel by a different road in the future. Please consider that even animals as small as mice may be of some service to you in the future."

The Elephant-King thought the mice request was entirely reasonable and granted it. More time passed and it came to be that a King of a nearby region ordered his soldiers to trap elephants for their ivory. Eventually, they trapped the Elephant-King and many in his herd. When he was all bound up the Elephant-King brooded upon how he could escape from the trap of certain death. Then he remembered the mice and realized that only they could help him now. So he somehow managed to get a baby-elephant to take his message to the mice with information on where he was being held with some of his followers. When the mice learned that they were needed to free the elephants, they gathered in the thousands and gnawed through the ropes, repaying their debt.

When Sense heard the story, he said "We will be happy to make friends with you. Please stay here by this lake with us and think of it as if it was your own home." So Speed joined in and the four friends lived and conversed together for many a day about religion, ethics, economics and many other important subjects.

Deer is Captured

One day, Speed did not show at their regular get-together. The three friends began to worry almost immediately and their fear only grew. They became convinced that Speed was in trouble. Then Sense and Smart said to Sight "You are the only one who can help in this emergency. Would you please fly up high and see what could have happened to Speed. And please return as soon as you are able with any news."

So Sight flew up high and circled in widening circles to see if he could find Speed. Quite soon he saw him caught in a strong deer trap made with thick ropes and braced with wood. When he alighted nearby, he asked Speed "How did you get caught in this trap?" But Speed responded with "There is no time for that. You make me happy just by your presence. *To have a friend when the end is near is itself a great boon.* Please forgive the impatience I showed in our discussions and likewise ask Sense and Smart to pardon me. Let only the memory of friendship live." To which Sight said "Feel no fear, Speed, while you have friends like us in your hour of need. I will return as fast as I can with Smart to gnaw through your bonds."

Then Sight flew back to the lake as fast as could and returned with Smart on his back. When the Mouse saw the Deer in captivity, he also asked "My friend, you always had a cautious bent and a shrewd eye, so how did you get caught?" And Speed answered with "Why ask? Fate does what it will. Who can fight an unseen enemy? Please quickly cut my bonds before the merciless hunter returns." "Not to worry", said Smart. I will start gnawing right away. But do tell me how you got caught for I might learn from your story." "OK, if you insist" said Speed. "This is the second time I have been made captive." "Tell me the story of the first time" requested Smart. So Speed told the story about his first captivity.

Speed Caught In a Snare

"When I was six months old I used to run ahead of my herd in high spirits and to show how fast I was. That is why I got the name Speed. I did not, however, yet know both ways that deer run: straight and leap. One day I lost sight of my herd, got really scared, and ran straight as fast as I could in the direction I thought the herd had gone. I didn't see the snare in front of me and got caught. The herd had seen it and simply leapt over it. I was too young and did not know how to leap properly. So I was captured.

"When the hunter came back and saw that I was still a fawn, he took pity on me. He took me home planning to give me as a pet to a young prince. The Prince treated me with great affection and I quickly became the court plaything passed from one to another, which I really did not like. Finally, when the rainy season was at its height, I cried out loudly in longing for my family. The poor Prince thought he had somehow been bewitched, for how could a deer say something in a language he could understand. He was so worried that he stopped eating and developed a fever and put all the blame on me. The courtiers took it out on me, beating me up as often as they could. I survived because my time was not yet up and a court priest took pity on me. He explained to the Prince that all animals talk but not aloud, in front of humans. 'You should not be afraid of the fawn. He simply misses his family.' So the Prince ordered his servants to take me back to the forest and set me free and he quickly recovered from his illness. That is the story of my first captivity and here I am ensnared again for *there is no avoiding fate*" said Speed.

At this point Sense joined them. He was so concerned about his friend Speed whom he had followed even though the going had been very hard. Seeing Sense arrive, the others were even more distressed. Smart spoke for all of them when he said "You should not have come. Here you will not be able to save yourself when the bonds are cut and the hunter is near. Speed will run away fast by leaps and bounds. Sight will fly up into a tree and even I will find a hole to slide into. What will you do when the hunter returns, which will be very shortly." To which Sense simply replied "*It is better to lose your life than your friends.*"

Of course, the hunter arrived just then and Smart's fears were realized. Bonds cut, Speed bounded off. He didn't see Smart and Sight who did exactly as Smart had predicted. Only Sense, the slow turtle, remained visible. The hunter, resigned to the loss of the deer, grabbed the turtle, tied his feet, slung it over a stick and carried him off. But when Smart saw what was happening, he bemoaned his fate "First came loss of property, then my followers fled from me, my own kind, and then I had to leave home and country, and now fate is planning to take away my friend. Ah me, the loss of my friend will be the death of me." By then Sight and Speed reached Smart and added their lament to his.

A few minutes had passed when Smart had an idea and said to the others "We might still have a chance of saving Sense. Speed, get to that pond there and play dead. Sight, you jump up and down on Speed's head and pretend to be plucking his eyes and make as loud squawking sounds as you can make. The hunter will turn back to look and be sure to think Speed is dead. He will be drawn back immediately by his greed, getting such a big catch without any effort. He will put Sense down on the ground while he goes for the deer and I will quickly gnaw at the turtle's ropes and free him to get to the pond before the Hunter knows what is happening. Speed, the minute you hear the splash, jump up and run for your life. Sight, you fly off, and I will seek a hole." The friends quickly and carefully carried out their plan. They all became quite invisible and to the hunter it seemed a conjurer's trick. Suddenly, he became afraid for his own life and left the woods as fast as he could, empty handed.

That is how the four friends got a new lease on life and they lived together in friendship for many, many years.

ACKNOWLEDGEMENTS

As I have noted elsewhere, the *Panchatantra* stories (literally Five Books) have been part of India's oral and scholarly tradition for at least two thousand years or more. They have been told and retold all over the world and have influenced many literary genres, particularly those containing animal characters and 'nesting stories' i.e. one story in another story in another story. Sometime towards the end of the twelfth century, the seminal version of the *Panchatantra* was written by Vishnusharma in Sanskrit and has formed the best known rendition ever since. It is comprised of a vast array of folk wisdom interspersed with eighty-five stories which collectively serve as a guide book of sorts on how to live a wise and good life. Many translations of the text are available in English and some selected stories have been published for young children. However, the entire collection has never been adapted for casual readers, whether teenagers or adults.

My goal is to make the core of the *Panchatantra* easily accessible to the English speaking world. I have delved deeply into three authoritative, literal, translations of the complete text of the *Panchatantra* from the original Sanskrit by three eminent scholars: Arthur W. Rider (1925), Chandra Rajan (1993) and Patrick Olivelle (1997). Their work represents the best of what serious academics have to offer. I am clearly indebted to them. Nevertheless, the original in its entirety remains rather difficult to register and enjoy for non-academics. I have used their translations to understand and stay as close to the original of the *Panchatantra* as possible. Beyond that, the way I have organized the five books for a lay audience, the telling of the stories, the language used, and the summary of the wisdom highlighted by the stories, are entirely mine.

I have read and re-read the stories in various forms over the last fifty years. I wish I had a way of publicly thanking all the authors I have read on the subject of the Panchatantra. Suffice it to say, their work taught me that these ancient stories are the essence of Indian wisdom and values that deserve a wide international audience.

Throughout this venture, my husband Michael has been my strongest backer, my sharpest critic, my meticulous editor, and my most longsuffering love. I cannot thank him enough. I also owe thanks to my children, Kieran and Sean, who never failed to point out that my stories were not PC enough for children, and to my friends, Roland, Judy and Jon, who did not hesitate to point out that my story-telling was too confusing even for adults. I hope they will see that I took their judgments seriously.

I hope that my enthusiasm for these stories is catching. Cheers.

Narindar Uberoi Kelly, March 26 2014

MORE TALL TALES OF OLD INDIA

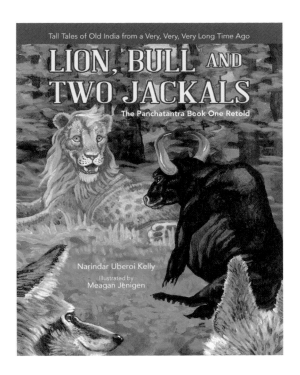

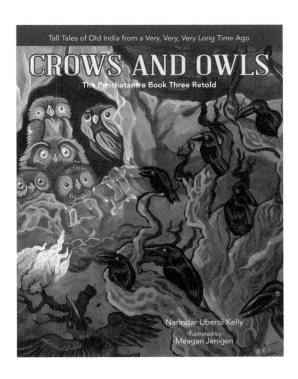

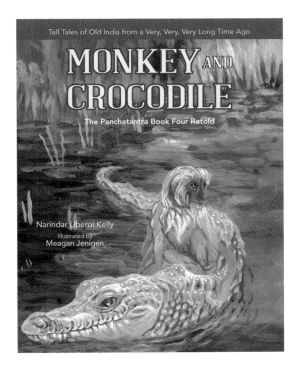

The Panchatantra Retold

Narindar Uberoi Kelly

Illustrated by Meagan Jenigen

CPSIA information can be obtained
at www.ICGtesting.com
Printed in the USA
BVIC01n1454220714
359734BV00002B/4